Caillou

My Book of Great Adventures

chouette

COOKIE JAR

Contents

Caillou

The Birthday Party

Adaptation from the animated series: Claire St-Onge
Illustrations: CINAR Animation

Today is Caillou's birthday. Caillou watches as Mommy puts icing on his birthday cake.

"Caillou, would you like to help me clean the bowl?" Mommy asks.

"Yes, please, Mommy!" says Caillou. He scrapes the icing from the bowl with the big spatula. He smiles as he licks at the sweet icing.

Rosie comes into the kitchen and
sees the yummy cake. ."I want some!"
she says.
"Let Rosie have a taste, Caillou," says
Daddy. He dips his finger into the
bowl.
"I thought you said that Caillou should
let *Rosie* have some," says Mommy.
Caillou giggles when he hears
Mommy scolding Daddy!

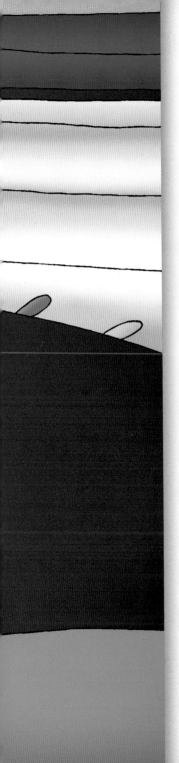

It's time for Caillou to open his present from Grandma. Caillou has told everyone that he wants a new dinosaur for his birthday.
Did Grandma remember?
Caillou opens the big box, hoping a dinosaur is inside. As soon as Caillou sees that the gift from Grandma is a sweater, he is disappointed.

Caillou hears the doorbell ring and
runs to the door.
"Clementine! Leo!" shouts Caillou.
Everyone is here now. The games
can begin.

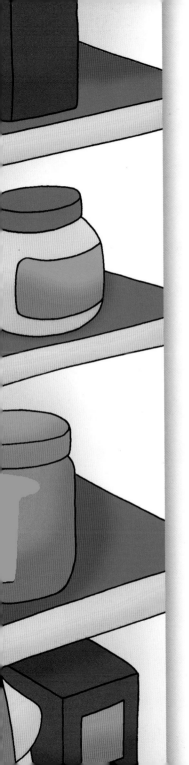

Daddy takes out the face-painting kit.
He starts to draw a circle around
Caillou's eye.
"Stay still just a little longer, Caillou.
I'm almost done," Daddy says.
"It feels funny, Daddy!" says Caillou.
He giggles at the tickly feeling of the
brush on his cheeks. He can't see the
whiskers Daddy is drawing on them.

Caillou, Rosie, Clementine, and Leo are having fun in the kitchen. There are treats to eat, and they all have painted faces. Caillou looks just like his cat, Gilbert!

Here comes Caillou's birthday cake!
"Happy birthday, Caillou!" everyone
shouts. Caillou can't wait to blow out
the candles.
"First you have to make a wish,
Caillou," says Grandma.
Caillou knows exactly what to wish
for-a new dinosaur! He takes a deep
breath and blows out the candles with
all his might.

Caillou has eaten all the cake he
can. Mommy and Daddy give him
a big box.
"Happy birthday, Caillou!" they say.
Caillou unwraps the box as fast as
he can.
"Wow! My dinosaur!" says Caillou,
hugging his new toy. "Thank you!"

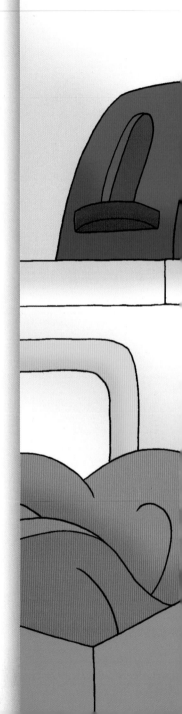

"Rosie! Look what you did!" says
Caillou, pointing to a big blob of ice
cream on his shirt.
"It's okay, Caillou," says Mommy.
"Rosie didn't do it on purpose."
"Here's a clean sweater for you
to wear," says Grandma, taking
Caillou's new sweater out of the box
and holding it up.

"Wow!" exclaims Caillou. He is
surprised to see that his new
birthday sweater has a dinosaur on it!
He quickly takes off his shirt and pulls
on the sweater.
"It's *another* birthday dinosaur!" says
Caillou, smiling. "This is my best
birthday ever!"

Caillou

Favorite T-shirt

Adaptation from the animated series: Jeanne Verhoye-Millet
Illustrations: CINAR Animation

"Catch the car, Teddy!"
Caillou has made up a new game.
He's rolling his toy cars down a ramp
made out of a long board.
Rosie walks into the room pulling her
toy ducky on a string.
"Can I play?" she asks.

"Okay," says Caillou. He turns to his little sister, and sees that she is wearing a T-shirt with teddy bears on it.
"No!" shouts Caillou. "That's my T-shirt! Take it off. It's mine!"
He is very upset.

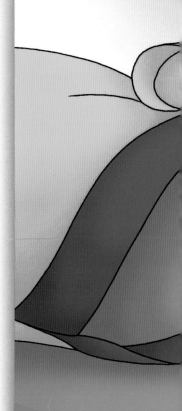

Mommy comes when she hears Caillou shouting. She tries to explain why Rosie is wearing Caillou's favorite T-shirt.

"Caillou, that T-shirt is too small for you, so I gave it to Rosie."

Caillou is so angry he is not listening to Mommy.

"It's not Rosie's! It's mine!" says Caillou with tears in his eyes.

"Okay, okay," says Mommy. "Rosie, let's go put on a different T-shirt."

Caillou puts on his teddy bear T-shirt,
but it's not easy. He has to wriggle
and squirm like a caterpillar.
"Hmm . . . Aargh . . . Ow!" he says
as his ears get stuck in the neck of
the shirt.
Finally, Caillou says happily, "See?
It's not too small!" He marches
around the room with his bare
tummy showing.

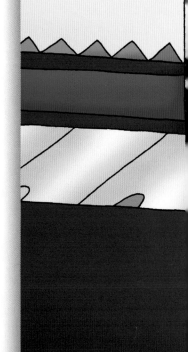

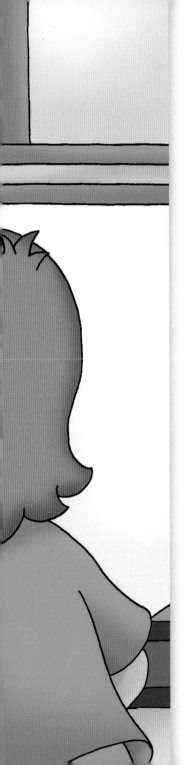

Rosie thinks Caillou looks very funny.
Maybe he's playing a new game.
She runs up to her brother and tickles
his tummy.
"Coochy-coo!" she says, giggling.
"Stop that," says Caillou. He knows
that the T-shirt used to cover his tummy
when he wore it.

Caillou stretches out to play with his cars, but his back gets cold and the carpet makes him feel itchy.
Caillou goes to his room. He doesn't want to play with his cars any more. He is too sad to do anything but sit with Teddy. Why did the T-shirt have to get too small?

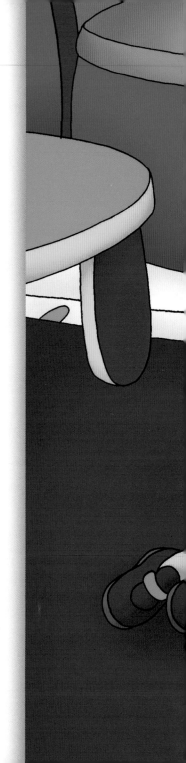

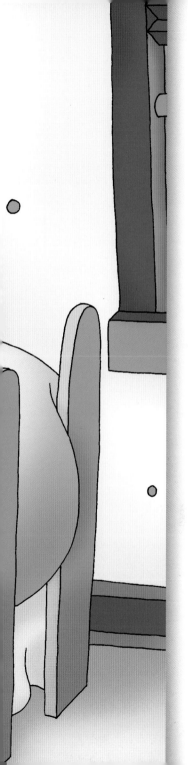

Mommy comes in and sits down
beside Caillou. She has a photo
album that she opens.
"Here's a picture of you on your
second birthday," she says. "You look
so cute and happy in your teddy bear
T-shirt."
Caillou looks at the picture. He nods
and says, "That's when I was little.
I had my teddy shirt."

Mommy understands why Caillou feels sad.

"Caillou, I'm sorry I gave your T-shirt to Rosie," she says. "I forgot how much you loved it. But now it's yours again. Even if you don't wear it, you can keep it as long as you want."

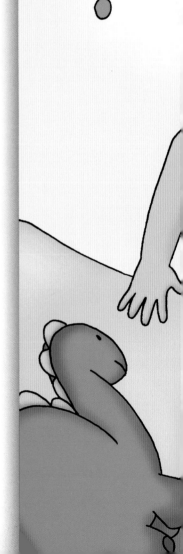

Caillou still loves his T-shirt. It's so
soft and cosy! But he knows he has
grown too big to wear it.
Caillou looks down at Teddy.
Suddenly, he knows what to do.
"I'm going to give it to Teddy,"
he says with a happy smile.
"Good idea, Caillou!" says Mommy.
She smiles too, as Caillou takes off
his favorite T-shirt and puts it on his
teddy bear.

Rosie comes into Caillou's room to find Mommy. Look who's wearing the T-shirt!
"Teddy's happy!" she giggles.
"Me too," says Caillou. He laughs and hugs Teddy in his teddy bear T-shirt.

Caillou

The Picnic

Adaptation from the animated series: Michel Bélair
Illustrations: CINAR Animation and adapted by Eric Sévgny

Caillou and his friend Leo are playing in the back seat of the car. Outside, the sky is cloudy and the wind twists the branches of the trees into strange shapes. The two boys are excited because they're on their way to the woods for a picnic. But it's taking so long to get there!

"We're almost there, kids," Mommy finally says. "Look, there's the parking lot!"

As soon as Daddy parks the car,
Caillou and Leo run outside and put
on their backpacks. They look up and
see the clouds racing across the sky.
They spot the picnic tables far in the
distance.

Mommy helps Caillou's baby sister
Rosie out of the car while Daddy gets
the picnic things out of the trunk.

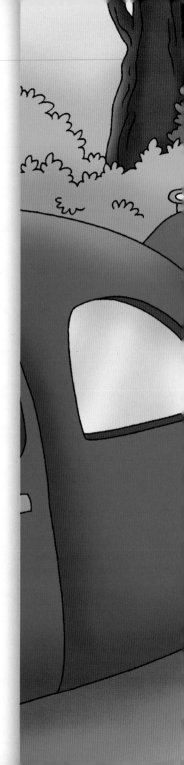

Like explorers, the group heads into
the woods. They walk single-file along
a winding path. The tall trees are filled
with birds calling out to each other.
Caillou and Leo are wide-eyed with
excitement as they lead the way.
The fresh air smells so good!
All of a sudden they stop. It's so quiet
they feel like they are all alone in the
forest.

"It's like the forest in your storybook about brave knights and dragons," Mommy says to Caillou.
"Yes, it is!" Caillou answers. Caillou and Leo smile at each other, ready to find adventure.

The two boys gobble down their lunch. They can't wait to go exploring. Caillou and Leo are already climbing to the top of a little hill. "Don't go too far, boys," says Daddy.

"Look at me," Leo shouts. He has
pulled a branch off an old, dried
tree trunk. He waves it in the air.
"I'm a brave knight. This is my sword!"
Caillou snaps off his own stick and
lifts it over his head.
"I have a sword too," he yells proudly.
"This is a big bad dragon," says Leo,
hitting the tree trunk with his branch.
"Yeah! We're fighting the bad
dragon," Caillou calls back, swinging
his stick.

Just then, the boys hear Mommy and Daddy calling, "Caillou! Leo! Come back now! We're leaving!"
The two friends run back to the picnic table. All the picnic things are packed and ready to go. Caillou feels a drop of rain fall on his nose.
Suddenly there's a crash of thunder.
"A dragon!" shouts Caillou.
"Let's get it!" says Leo.

Caillou and Leo run ahead of the group, waving their swords.
It's raining harder and harder. As the thunder-dragon's roars get louder, Rosie starts to cry.
They find a little cave where they can all huddle inside, taking shelter from the storm. But Rosie is still afraid, and can't stop crying.

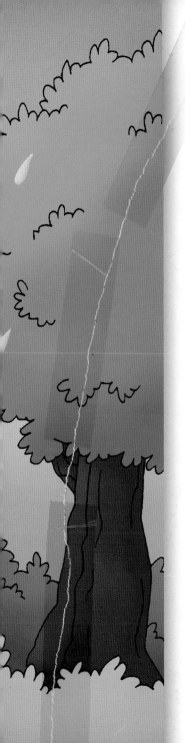

"Look, Rosie," Caillou tells his sister.
"I'm a brave knight. Here's my sword."
"Me too," Leo adds quickly. "We'll
fight the dragon!"
"Yeah!" Caillou points his sword at
the big black clouds in the sky. "We'll
protect you," he says.

All of a sudden, the thunder rolls away
into the distance, the rain stops, and the
sun peeks out from behind the clouds.
Rosie smiles. Caillou and Leo are proud
of themselves, as they once more take
the lead back to the parking lot.
"Hey, my brave knights," Daddy says
with a smile. "Are you sure there are
no more dragons around?"
Leo and Caillou laugh and wave
their wooden swords. "Don't worry,
Daddy, we scared them away!"

Caillou

At the Market

Adaptation from the animated series: Marion Johnson
Illustrations: CINAR Animation and adapted by Eric Sévigny

Caillou doesn't want to get out
of bed.
"Look!" says Daddy. "It's snowing!"
Caillou runs to look out the window.
"Wow! Can we make a snowman?"
"Let's get dressed first," Daddy tells
him. "Then we'll see."

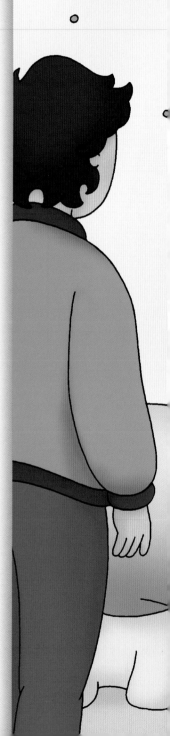

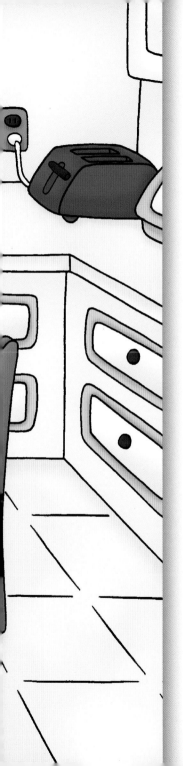

Caillou tries to pour his cereal,
but nothing comes out.
"There's no cereal," he tells Mommy.
"We'll get some at the market," she
says. "We have to shop for things to
make a special surprise cake."
A cake! "Yay!" shouts Caillou.

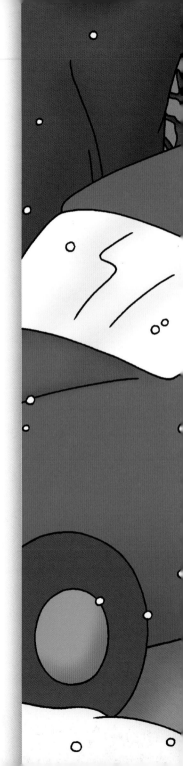

Caillou puts on his coat and boots.
Outside, the snowflakes tickle his face.
He sticks out his tongue and catches
some of them.
"Can we make a snowman?"
"Yes, Caillou," Mommy answers.
"But we have to go to the market first."

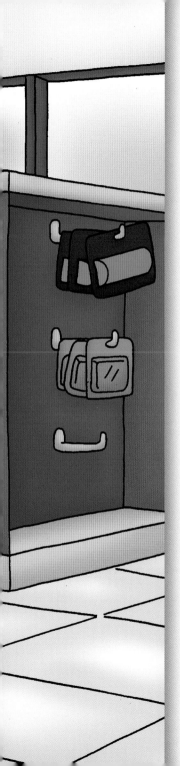

When they get to the market,
Mommy puts Rosie in the seat of
the grocery cart.
Caillou wants to go for a ride, too.
Mommy lifts him into the cart.
"Let's go! We have lots of shopping
to do."

Caillou and Rosie help Mommy find
the things she needs.
Caillou takes a bag of cookies off
the shelf.
"These are good!" he says.
"We're having a special surprise
cake," Mommy reminds him.
"So we don't need cookies, too."
Caillou really wants the cookies,
but he puts them back.

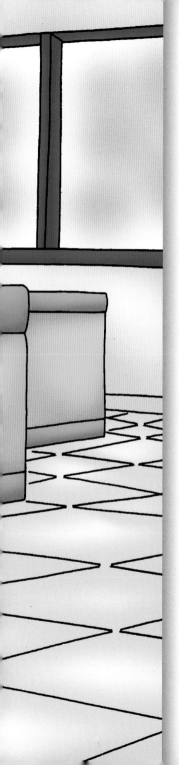

At the checkout counter, Mommy helps Caillou and Rosie get out of the cart.
"Caillou," she says, "Please watch Rosie for me."
Caillou holds Rosie's hand.
But he is thinking about the cookies.
He decides to go and get them.

Caillou goes up and down the aisles,
looking for the cookies.
Suddenly he stops and looks around.
He can't see Mommy.
Caillou is lost!
"Mommy!" cries Caillou. "Where
are you, Mommy?"

There she is! Mommy looks worried.
"What happened, Caillou?"
"You went away!" Caillou sobs.
"No, *you* went away," says
Mommy. She gives him a big hug.
"But I'm very glad we found you.
Let's go home."

Caillou says, "Mommy, I was lost."
"I know, Caillou," says Mommy.
"But you're home now. And it's time
to make the special surprise cake."
"But I want to make a snowman,"
says Caillou.

Mommy smiles. "We will make
a snowman... here in the kitchen!"
Mommy bakes the cake and covers
it with snowy white icing. Caillou
and Rosie decorate it with candy.
"Look," says Caillou happily.
"The special surprise cake is a
special surprise snowman!"

Caillou

At the Beach

Adaptation from the animated series: Marion Johnson
Illustrations: CINAR Animation and adapted by Eric Sévigny

It's summer vacation, and Caillou
is going to the beach.
He can't wait to see what the
ocean is like.
At last Daddy parks the car.
Caillou jumps out and runs down
to look at the water.

"Wow!" shouts Caillou. "The ocean!"
The ocean goes on forever. It's the
biggest thing Caillou has ever seen.
"Caillou, it's very sunny and that
means sunscreen," says Mommy.

Caillou giggles and tries to get away,
but Mommy holds on tight.
She covers him all over with sunscreen.
It tickles!
When Mommy is finally finished,
Caillou runs down the beach.

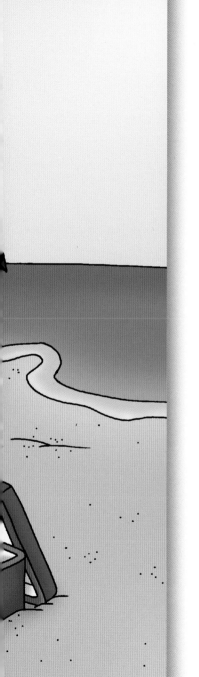

Daddy sets up the umbrella, and
Mommy puts Rosie down in the shade.
Caillou doesn't want to sit in the
shade. He wants to do something!
"Anyone want to go swimming?"
asks Daddy.
"Me! Me!" Caillou jumps up and
grabs Daddy's hand.
They run together into the water.

Brrrr! "The water is cold," says Caillou.
"It's all right once you get used
to it," Daddy tells him.
Suddenly a big wave knocks
Daddy down.
Caillou laughs because Daddy
looks funny.
Then a wave knocks Caillou down.
Caillou giggles. This is fun!

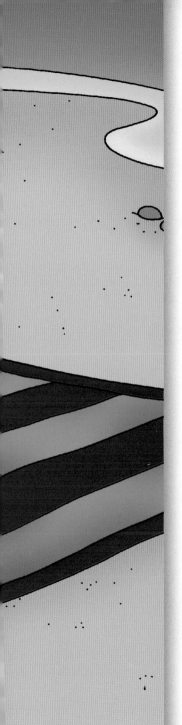

Caillou is eating a sandwich for lunch.
He drinks some lemonade. Yummy!
Caillou picks up his sandwich and
takes a big bite, but now it's full of
sand. So he puts it down.
A seagull flies by and grabs the
sandy sandwich!
"Hey, come back!" exclaims Caillou.

After lunch, Caillou goes exploring
along the beach.
He finds a little pool of sea water.
He lies down to take a closer look.
Look, there are all kinds of sea
animals swimming in it!

Caillou runs when he hears
Mommy calling, "Want to build
a sandcastle, Caillou?"
Caillou shows Rosie how
to make towers.
"Look, Rosie," he says. "You take
the pail and go like this."
Rosie giggles and claps her hands.
Sandcastles are the most fun of all!

Suddenly Caillou feels water
splashing him.
The ocean has moved closer,
and the castle is washing away!
"What happened?" asks Caillou.
"The tide makes the water get
higher and lower," Mommy
explains. "Right now, the tide is
coming in. And that means it's
time for us to go."

Mommy and Daddy gather up all their things and head for the car. "Don't worry, Caillou," Mommy says. "We can come back tomorrow and build another sandcastle."

Caillou smiles. "I want to come back tomorrow and the next day and the next day. This is the best vacation ever!"

Caillou

At the Amusement Park

Adaptation from the animated series: Marion Johnson
Illustrations: CINAR Animation and adapted by Eric Sévigny

Caillou has been riding in the car for a long, long time. When will they get to the amusement park?
"Are we there yet?" he asks Daddy.
"There yet?" Rosie repeats.
Daddy laughs. "Hold your horses. I think I see the amusement park up ahead."

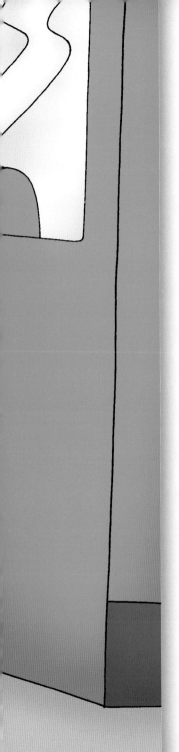

Caillou runs to get on the first ride.
"Stand next to the board, Caillou,"
says Daddy.
"Why?"
"You can't go on the River Ride if
you're too little," Daddy explains.
Caillou is just big enough!

Daddy and Caillou ride the
waves together.
"It's kind of scary, isn't it?" Daddy
says to Caillou.
"Yes," Caillou agrees. He's glad that
Daddy is also a little scared.
Soon Caillou is having too much fun
to be nervous. And so is Daddy.

"Here's the snack bar," says Daddy.
"Let's have lunch!"
Caillou and Rosie each get a hot dog.
What's for dessert? Daddy holds out
two big sticks of cotton candy.
"Cotton candy isn't really that good
for us," Mommy says.

The cotton candy melts in Caillou's mouth! Daddy has cotton candy for Mommy, too.

"Are you sure you don't want some?" he asks.

"It does look good," Mommy says, laughing and taking a taste.

"I guess it's okay once in a while."

After lunch, they take a ride on
the Ferris wheel.
The car rocks gently as it climbs all
the way to the top.
Caillou looks down.
"Mommy! Daddy! Look!" he shouts.
"You can see everything from up here!"

"There's the River Ride," says Daddy.
"And the merry-go-round,"
adds Mommy.
"And the snack bar," Caillou laughs.
Rosie giggles. "Yay!"

It's almost time to go home.
Suddenly Caillou sees something
really exciting — a huge teddy bear!
"Daddy, Daddy, look! Can we win
that prize?" he asks.
"Hmmm, you have to throw all three
hoops over that wooden block," says
Daddy. "Let's try!"

Caillou goes first.
All of his hoops fall on the ground.
The game is really hard.
Then Daddy takes his turn.
Caillou really, really wants
Daddy to win the big teddy bear.
One, two, three—all of Daddy's
hoops land on the block!

"What did you like the best,
Caillou?" asks Mommy on the way
home. "Was it the Ferris wheel?
Or the River Ride?"
Caillou shakes his head.
"I know," Mommy says. "It was the
teddy bear."
Caillou smiles. "The teddy bear is the
best of all!"

We acknowledge the financial support of the Government of Canada through the Canada Book Fund for our publishing activities.

Canadian Patrimoine
Heritage canadien

We acknowledge the support of the Ministry of Culture and Communications of Quebec and SODEC for the publication and promotion of this book.

SODEC
Québec

Bibliothèque et Archives nationales du Québec and
Library and Archives Canada cataloguing in publication

Main entry under title :

Caillou : my book of great adventures

(Treasury collection)
Issued also in French under title: Caillou : mon grand livre d'aventures.
Content: Caillou : the birthday party – Caillou : favorite T-shirt – Caillou : the picnic – Caillou : at the market – Caillou : at the beach – Caillou : at the amusement park.

For children aged 3 ans up.

ISBN 978-2-89450-713-1

1. Child development - Juvenile literature. 2. Self-realization - Juvenile literature.

HQ767.9.C3413 2009   j305.231   C2008-942126-4

Legal deposit: 2009

Printed in Shenzhen, China
10 9 8 7 6 5 4 3 2 CHO1761 NOV2010